THE BOXCAR CHILDREN

CREATED BY
GERTRUDE CHANDLER WARNER

BOOK
147

THE ROBOT RANSOM

WITHDRAWN

ILLUSTRATED BY
ANTHONY VanARSDALE

ALBERT WHITMAN & COMPANY
CHICAGO, ILLINOIS

Contents

Robot Ready

Benny Alden knelt on the floor of the boxcar, nose to nose with a one-foot-tall robot. "Hi, DogBot!" he said.

"*Arf!*" The robot barked and rolled back and forth on its wheels.

Six-year-old Benny laughed. "I see why you call it DogBot. It doesn't look like a dog, but it barks like one!"

His brother Henry grinned. "We modeled the robot after a search and rescue dog. The barking is just for fun." At fourteen, Henry was the oldest of the Alden siblings.

Twelve-year-old Jessie nodded. "Search and rescue dogs affected our design. But our robot doesn't have to look like a real dog."

The robot backed away from Benny and began exploring the room. When DogBot got to a wall, it turned. Soon the robot dog got close to the Aldens' real dog, a wire fox terrier named Watch. DogBot let out another friendly "*Arf!*" Watch just backed into a corner and growled.

Violet, who was ten, hurried to give Watch a hug. "Don't worry. We would never replace you with a robot dog!" Watch licked her face and then turned to look suspiciously at DogBot. The children laughed.

"Watch knows that's not a real dog!" said Benny.

Henry checked the time on his phone. "Is everyone ready to leave?"

"We have the robot and the laptop," said Jessie.

"Our suitcases are in the house," said Violet. "I helped Benny pack."

"All right," said Henry, picking up DogBot. "Say good-bye to the boxcar for a few days."

The boxcar was their clubhouse, and they loved hanging out inside it. But it had once been their home. After the children's parents had died, they'd heard their grandfather was mean, so they ran away.

They found a boxcar in the woods and decided to live inside. The Aldens had many adventures before they finally met their grandfather. He turned out to be very kind, and he brought them to his home to stay. Now they all lived together, with the boxcar in the backyard. They still had many adventures.

"We'll have to say good-bye to Watch too." Violet gave the dog another hug. "We'll miss you, but you wouldn't like being around all those robots."

"Thousands and thousands of robots!" said Benny. "I can't wait."

"Well, hundreds of robots anyway." Henry led the way back to the house. "This is a regional Robot Roundup. A dozen high school robotics teams will be competing. We're one of ten middle school teams." Henry and Jessie had joined the Greenfield Middle School team that year.

"That sounds like a tough contest," said Violet.

Benny skipped ahead toward the house and called back, "Henry and Jessie can win."

Henry smiled. "Thanks. Winning would be nice. But no matter what happens, we've already learned a lot."

"It has been fun," said Jessie. "We're lucky that our team members have so much experience." As the children went through the back door of the house, the front doorbell rang. "That must be Naomi and Rico now!"

The Aldens hurried to answer the door, where Jessie introduced her teammates to Violet and Benny. "Naomi and Rico have done this competition for two years," she said.

Naomi had dark skin and a puffy halo of black hair. She said, "Each team has four students. Our old teammates are in high school this year. We sure are glad Henry and Jessie joined us."

Rico was tall, with tan skin and dark hair falling into his eyes. "We need a good team if we're going to beat Silver City." Watch came up and sniffed at Rico's knee, making him jump. Then he bent down to pet the dog.

"The Greenfield STEAM Team can do it!" said Naomi.

Violet was often shy with strangers, but Naomi was wearing a purple shirt. Purple was Violet's favorite color. She immediately liked the older girl, so she said, "That's a good team name. I'm glad you included Art along with Science, Technology, Engineering, and Math. I like STEAM better than STEM."

"Oh, I get it now," said Benny. "STEAM comes from the first letters of those other words."

"That's right, Benny," Jessie said proudly. Then she turned to Naomi. "Violet is an artist."

"That's great," Naomi said. "Art is an important part of science and engineering. Maybe you'll join the robotics club in a couple of years."

Grandfather entered the room. Henry introduced him to Naomi and Rico. "Thank you for offering to drive us," said Rico.

Grandfather nodded. "I have business near Port Elizabeth. We'll stay at the hotel together. I can drop you off and then take care of my work. It will be fun for Violet and Benny to see all the robots too. Shall we go?"

Everyone double-checked that they had their luggage. Benny held up a bulging tote bag. "I'm bringing lots of snacks! Watching robots makes me hungry."

Henry laughed. "Everything makes you hungry, Benny."

"Snacks are a good idea," said Naomi. "The conference has a lot to see. It can be tiring."

"I thought it was a contest, not a *con-for*...that other thing," Benny said.

"Conference," said Jessie. "The contest is part of the conference. There are also displays and talks. Businesses will have booths to show off their new robots."

Grandfather said, "A conference is a big meeting with many people. They expect about a thousand people each day at this Robot Roundup. Now get yourself and your snacks into the car." He patted Benny on the back.

Once they were on the road, Violet turned to Rico. "You said you want to beat the Silver City team. What about the other teams?"

"Sure," said Rico. "But the Greenfield STEAM Team and the Silver City Gearheads are rivals."

"We get along with most of the teams," Naomi explained. "Building robots is mainly about learning and having fun. But it's different with the Gearheads."

"Tell them what happened last year," said Henry.

Rico nodded. "The Silver City team is very competitive, especially this boy named Logan. He can get pretty insulting."

"He doesn't have the right spirit for the Robot Roundup," Naomi said. "But that's not the worst part. Last year, we won fair and square, but Logan complained. He said the judges hadn't given us the right score."

Violet stared at her with wide eyes. "What happened?"

Naomi shrugged. "The judges stayed with their decision. We got the trophy and the prize money. But Logan and the Gearheads kept saying bad things about us. It took some of the fun out of winning."

Jessie made a face. "I'm not looking forward to meeting him."

"We'll avoid him as much as possible," said Henry. "We have a good robot, and we play fair."

"You have a great DogBot!" said Benny, reaching over to pet the plastic robot.

The others chuckled. "That's the right spirit,"

said Grandfather. "We're nearing Port Elizabeth. Henry, can you help me find the exit?"

Henry used the map on his phone to find the best way to the hotel. After a few minutes, they pulled up at the door and piled out. They carried their bags into the lobby and waited while Grandfather checked in.

Jessie looked around the lobby. "It's time to meet Coach Kaleka, but I don't see him yet."

Henry, Rico, and Naomi also looked around the lobby. A few people sat in chairs, while others came and went. Naomi said, "I don't see Coach. But there's the Silver City team!"

A short woman with big glasses was talking to four children. One of them, a boy about Henry's age, glanced around the room. When he spotted their group by the check-in desk, he walked over. "Look, it's the Greenfield *daydream* team," he said. "Because you're dreaming if you think you can beat us."

Naomi rolled her eyes. "Hello, Logan."

"Are these your new team members?" Logan pointed at Violet and Benny. "I guess even little kids could do better than you."

"Hey, I could make a good robot!" Benny said. Violet simply ducked behind Jessie. She didn't want any trouble.

Henry stepped forward. "I'm Henry and this is my sister Jessie. We're the new members of the Greenfield STEAM Team. We're looking forward to a fun, fair competition with good sportsmanship."

Logan snickered at that. Before he could speak, Grandfather turned from the desk and handed the children keys. "Here you are, rooms two twenty-two and two twenty-four. Let's go unpack."

"What about Coach?" Naomi asked. "Should we wait for him?"

"Is he usually on time?" Grandfather asked.

Naomi and Rico looked at each other and shrugged. Rico said, "He's been late for our meetings, but only by a few minutes. We haven't done any trips with him before."

Henry asked the hotel clerk, "Has Mr. Kaleka checked in yet?" He spelled the name for her.

The woman checked the computer. "No one by that name has a reservation this weekend, and the hotel is all booked up. Lots of people are coming for the Robot Roundup."

"Thank you," said Henry, turning back to his family and teammates. "Maybe Coach is staying at a different hotel."

"I'll text him and let him know our room numbers," suggested Rico.

"Good plan," said Grandfather. "Let's go to our rooms so we're not in the way here."

They grabbed their bags and headed down the hallway. Henry glanced back, but Logan had disappeared. So had his teammates and coach.

At their rooms, Henry pushed open the door that said 222. Something made a soft scuffling sound.

"What was that noise?" asked Rico.

Henry stepped into the room. "There's a piece of paper on the floor. The door pushed it back." He picked up the white paper. Words were written on it in black marker.

Greenfield, Go Home!

Artificial Intelligence

The next morning, the children gathered in the hotel lobby. Henry noticed a computer that guests could use. Next to it was a stack of white paper to feed into a printer. A jar on the table held pencils, markers, and a pair of scissors. "Look," Henry said. "Whoever left that message for us might have gotten the paper from here."

"I'm sure it was Logan," said Rico, hugging DogBot to his chest.

"Maybe," Jessie agreed. "But the person used normal white paper and a black marker. We don't have many clues."

"Just the handwriting," said Henry. "Anyway, let's forget it and enjoy the day. Has anyone heard from Coach yet?"

Rico pulled out his phone and stared at it. "Nothing. I texted him last night and this morning."

"He's probably waiting for you all at the conference," Grandfather said. "It isn't far, so we can walk over."

The group walked a few blocks to the convention center. They entered a wide hallway with check-in tables set up along one side.

They found the table that had a sign saying E–H and stood in line. Benny said, "H for *Henry*, but what about the rest of you?"

Henry chuckled. "We're in this line because *G* is for *Greenfield*, our team name. We sign in by team."

"If you get separated, this is a good place to meet," said Grandfather.

"Don't they have someplace with food?" Benny asked. "I'd rather meet there!"

Henry ruffled Benny's shiny brown hair. "They do have a food court. We'll go there for lunch. But if you get lost before then, come here. We'll find you here, or you can ask the staff for help."

"All right," said Benny. "I have my snacks with

me anyway."

Everyone got their badges. The team members' badges had their names and Greenfield STEAM Team on them. Violet's and Benny's said Visitor. Grandfather said good-bye and left to take care of his business. The children headed to the main hall for the conference.

Inside, they stopped and looked around. Hundreds of people filled the room. And that wasn't all.

"Look!" said Benny, jumping up and down with excitement. "It's a real, live robot!"

Jessie laughed. "Well, it's real anyway. I don't think it's alive though. Let's take a look." They joined a crowd clustered around a platform. On the platform stood a shiny white robot as tall as a person. It had smooth arms and legs, and a normal-looking head with eyes, ears, and a mouth. A man was talking about the robot. "This robot can move much like a human," he said.

Then the man reached out and shoved the robot. The robot fell forward, landing on its hands and knees. The crowd gasped. After a few seconds, the robot stood up again.

Benny said, "I'm surprised the robot didn't blast that guy with laser beams!"

Naomi smiled at Benny. "Robots do use lasers but not the dangerous kind. They use lasers to sense what's around them. Some robots can 'see' the room around them using lasers."

"Knocking the robot down seems mean," Violet whispered.

"Robots don't have feelings," said Rico. "The man was just showing how the robot could get up again. It's much harder than it looks. That's why we used four wheels on our robot. Balancing on two legs is very difficult."

Benny looked down at his own legs. "It doesn't seem that hard."

"You have lots of little muscles in your legs," said Naomi. "Plus, your inner ear tells you how to balance. And your brain sends signals to your muscles. Everything works together. The human body is incredibly complex."

Benny turned to Violet. "Did you hear that? I'm complex!"

Jessie grinned. "You sure are. Right now the

best robots are about as skilled and smart as a two-year-old. The people making robots can't make something as complex as you."

They walked through the room, looking at all the displays. Some of the robots had human shapes. Others did not. Some made beeping noises or flashed lights. Some spoke English.

Violet said, "That first one we saw, the robot that fell down, he looked like a real robot. Some of these other things look like computers or machines."

"Robots come in many shapes and sizes," Naomi explained. "Any machine that can do things on its own is a robot. The ones that look like humans are called androids. But not all robots look like humans. Factories use robotic arms to move heavy objects. Then there are drones, which are robots that fly. Some cars are robots too—they can drive themselves."

Rico pointed to a display with pictures of a big cart on red sand. "That's the rover that explores Mars. It can drive through the desert and climb over rocks. It can even test the soil to learn about it—all without a human within thousands of miles."

"Some robots are controlled by people," said Benny, pointing at a girl using a remote control to move a truck. "But not all of them have people telling them what to do."

"That's right," said Naomi. "Some robots work all on their own. And some can even learn new things on their own. That's called artificial intelligence, or AI."

"Why didn't you make one like that?" Benny asked.

Naomi laughed. "Because it's really hard. Maybe one day we will make an android that can walk like a person and answer questions. But that wasn't our goal this time."

"Every year the Robot Roundup has a special challenge," Jessie said. "This year the middle school theme is When Disaster Strikes. We needed to build a robot that could help during a disaster."

"You mean like when Benny forgets to clean his room?" Violet teased.

"Sorry, Benny. I haven't seen any room-cleaning robots," said Jessie. "We were thinking about problems like earthquakes. People use search and rescue dogs to help find survivors. But sometimes it's not safe for people or dogs to go near a disaster area. That's when robots can be used to save lives."

Violet patted DogBot's head. "That sounds like a very good use for a robot."

"Speaking of our DogBot," said Henry, "we should drop him off at the staging area. It's crowded in here, and DogBot is built from lots of small pieces. If he gets dropped or bumped, pieces could come off." Henry led the way to the side of the large hall.

Temporary walls about ten feet high blocked off rooms for competing robots. Banners marked the places for each group to leave their robots.

"This way," said Henry, waving the others toward the middle school staging area. But as they approached the doorway, an android robot about as tall as Benny blocked the entrance. Large yellow eyes blinked at the children. A female voice came from the robot. "Good morning. I am the Sentry Android Robot Assistant. But you may call me SARA." Lights blinked in the robot's mouth as it spoke. "Only contestants are allowed inside this area."

"I'm a contestant," said Henry.

The robot's head turned slightly to look at him.

The eyes blinked. "Welcome, Henry Alden." Next the face turned to Jessie. "Welcome, Jessie Alden."

"How does it know your names?" Violet whispered. "That's creepy."

The robot turned its head toward her and blinked. "That is not a very nice thing to say."

Violet clapped her hand over her mouth, blushing. "Sorry!" She backed away.

The robot greeted Rico and Naomi by name. "The Greenfield STEAM Team may enter. Visitors must wait outside."

"Is somebody controlling it?" Benny asked.

Rico turned to Violet and Benny. "Don't worry," he said. "There must be an electronic chip in our ID badges that sends a signal to the robot. That's how it knows who we are."

Violet frowned at the robot. "Then it doesn't know my name. I'm glad."

"I don't see Coach anywhere," said Jessie.

"Maybe he's inside," said Naomi. "Let's go check."

"Wait for us here," Henry told Violet and Benny. "We'll drop off DogBot, and then we can look at more displays."

As the team went into the room, Benny stood face-to-face with SARA. "Do you know who I am?" he asked.

"You are not a registered team member," the robot said.

"That's true." Benny tried to think of more questions for the robot. "What's your favorite food?"

"Computer chips," SARA answered.

"That's funny," said Benny. "How old are you?"

SARA said, "I am thirteen months and four days old."

"You're just a baby!" exclaimed Benny.

SARA blinked at him. "Robots do not have babies, silly."

Violet pulled Benny away from the android. She whispered, "Naomi said robots don't have feelings. But this robot sure acts like she does!"

Meanwhile, the older children looked around inside the room. About a dozen students and a few adults were chatting. Ten tables were set up around the sides of the room. Each table had a sign with a team name on it. So far, about half of the tables had robots on them.

"Wow," said Jessie. "Some of these look really neat. I can't wait to see them in action."

"There's our spot," said Rico, crossing the room. But when he got to the table, he jumped back and gasped. The others hurried over.

They all looked down at the table. A propped-up sign read Greenfield STEAM Team. But a yellow sticky note sat on the table in front of the sign. The sticky note had words written in red marker. The children had to lean close to read the words.

Greenfield doesn't deserve to win!

CHAPTER 3

Strange Encounters

"Who would leave a mean note like that?" Jessie asked.

Rico grabbed the note and crumpled it in his hand. "Look over there," he said. "The Silver City team is here. I'll bet Logan left the note."

Naomi put her hands on her hips and glared at Logan. "I'm not afraid of him." She marched across the room and tapped Logan on the shoulder.

Logan turned and grinned at her. "What's the matter? You really look like you're *steam*-ing."

"Enough with the jokes," said Naomi. "You can't get us to quit that way."

"How can I get you to quit?" Logan asked.

"You can't!" Naomi said.

Rico held out his hand with the crumpled note. "You can have this back."

Logan's eyebrows rose as he looked at the sticky note. "Why would I want that? What is it?"

"It says we don't deserve to win," snapped Naomi.

"Imagine that!" said Logan. "Someone thinks you don't deserve to win. Here's a hint—*everyone* thinks that."

"You're always trying to cause trouble," Naomi said.

Logan shook his head. "You're the ones who caused trouble last year, with your cheating."

"We did not cheat!" Naomi and Rico said at the same time.

Jessie spoke gently, trying to calm everyone. "I'm sure they would not cheat. We all just want to have fun and do well."

"Cheating is a big accusation," Henry added. "You should not make that claim unless you have proof."

"Maybe they didn't cheat," said Logan. "But it still wasn't fair. Our robot did better in the trials. Your robot was scored wrong. Your team should have lost!"

Naomi lifted her chin. "The judges disagreed with you. We won last year, and we'll win again this year!"

"We'll see about that!" said Logan. "You should be kicked out of the competition forever. Just like your last coach!"

Rico hunched his shoulders and glanced around the room. "What our old coach did has nothing to do with us," he said. "We have a new coach now."

Logan shrugged. "You're as bad as he was. You should withdraw from the contest." He pointed at the note. "Everyone thinks so. But if you won't drop out, we'll beat you this year."

"Come on. Let's go," said Henry. "There's no point in arguing about this."

Rico turned away at once. Naomi looked like she had more to say to Logan. Jessie touched her friend's arm and said, "Violet and Benny are waiting. Let's visit the rest of the displays and enjoy ourselves."

Finally Naomi nodded. They ignored Logan and his teammates as they left the room. Outside, they joined Violet and Benny. Violet looked at their unhappy faces and asked what was wrong.

"Logan is what's wrong," said Naomi.

"Don't let him bother you," Jessie said. "He can't really do anything to us."

Rico was still holding the sticky note. He flattened it out and looked at it. "I hope Logan will be happy with leaving notes. What if he tries to break our robot?"

Henry glanced back into the room. "I don't see how he can. Someone would see him."

"Surely he wouldn't do anything that bad," Jessie said. "We don't know for sure that Logan even left this note."

"Another note?" Violet asked.

Jessie pointed at paper. "This one is different," she said.

"The note last night was on white paper," said Benny. "This one is on small yellow paper. The other one had black writing. This is red."

"That's right," Henry said. "It could mean two different people wrote the notes. Or maybe the same person just used different materials."

"What about the handwriting?" Jessie asked.

Henry studied the note. "Look at the way the

person wrote the letter *i*," he said. "Instead of a dot, there's a tiny circle on top. I don't remember that on the one from last night. But I threw that note away. The cleaners will probably empty the wastebasket before we get back."

"We need a sample of Logan's handwriting," said Naomi.

"How are we supposed to get that?" Rico asked. "He won't just give it to us."

"He sounded like he was telling the truth when he said it wasn't him," said Jessie. "Did you notice how he said *everyone* thinks we should lose? He seemed glad he wasn't the only one."

"But he is the only one," Naomi said. "We haven't had trouble with anyone else."

Rico scratched his head. "Could it be someone playing a joke on us? Coach Kaleka has a weird sense of humor sometimes. I don't always get his jokes."

"The note isn't very funny," said Jessie. "It doesn't seem like it could possibly be a joke. But I do wonder where Coach is."

Rico pulled out his phone. "He still hasn't answered my text. I'll try calling him." Half a minute later, he said, "It rang a bunch of times and then went to voice mail."

"I'm starting to get worried about him," said Jessie.

"It is strange," said Henry. "But I don't think we need to worry. He could be here but not be able to hear his phone. We don't really need him yet, since we don't compete until Sunday. Let's ignore Logan and concentrate on having fun."

"Good idea," said Jessie. "Today I want to enjoy myself. The competition is going to be exciting, but kind of scary too. A lot of people will be watching us and DogBot."

"I really want to win now," Rico said.

Naomi nodded. "We can't let Logan beat us this year!" She looked at Henry and Jessie. "This is the third time Rico and I are competing against Silver City. It sure would be nice to go home with the trophy."

"And the prize money," said Rico. "Four hundred dollars!"

"We'll do our best," said Henry. "We're not going to withdraw from the contest just because the Silver

City team are sore losers. But worrying won't help."

"I'm worried," Benny said.

Jessie put her arm around Benny. "What are you worried about?"

Benny patted his stomach. "I'm worried they'll be out of food before we get our lunch!"

They all chuckled. Henry said, "I'd like to look around a little more before we get lunch. How about breaking into your snack bag?"

Benny nodded and passed around granola bars. After their quick snack, the children went back through the main hall. Booths showed off all types of robots. Some were simply toys. Others could do work, such as moving boxes or helping people in wheelchairs.

A man in one booth said, "Someday everyone will have robots! And not just one robot. Every family will have a dozen robots. They'll cook and clean for you. They'll answer commands. They'll be friends."

"I'd like to have a robot friend," said Benny.

"Not me!" said Violet. "I like people. And animals."

A stage was set up for bigger demonstrations. A

team of waist-high robots played a game of soccer. They were very slow, but it was fun to watch them march around the field and kick the ball.

Finally Benny said, "My tummy is telling me it's time for lunch!"

The others agreed. They wove through the crowd, heading for the food court. As they walked, Violet spotted someone wearing a green shirt with black letters. It looked the same as the Greenfield STEAM Team T-shirts. "Is that your coach?" she asked.

"Where?" Naomi stretched her neck to look. "Hey, that's not Coach Kaleka. That's our old coach."

Henry said, "Logan mentioned your old coach was kicked out. What did he mean?"

Rico kept his voice low as he explained. "Coach Thompson got in trouble with the school. He joined a competition for fighting robots."

"He fought a robot?" Benny's eyes were big. "Wow!"

Naomi giggled. "Not quite. They have contests where the robots battle against each other. The goal is to destroy the other robot."

Rico said, "It's exciting to watch, but the school said it didn't set a good example."

"Plus, he used our robot," said Naomi. "It was school property. He lost the battle, and the robot was destroyed."

"That's too bad," said Henry. "It's tough that he got fired from coaching because of it though."

Naomi nodded. "He was a good coach. He knew a lot about robots. Coach Kaleka is nice, but he doesn't have much experience." She looked over at her old coach and waved to him. "Let's say hi."

Mr. Thompson came toward them slowly. He put one hand over his ID badge and fiddled with it nervously. "Hello, Rico, Naomi." He did not smile, and he kept glancing around, avoiding their gazes.

"It's nice to see you," Naomi said. "These are our new teammates."

"I know," Mr. Thompson said. "Jessie and Henry Alden."

Jessie and Henry exchanged a look. How did he know their names? They had never met him.

"What are you doing at the conference?" Rico asked.

Mr. Thompson's face went red, and he clenched his ID badge tightly. "I can be here. They might have fired me from coaching, but they can't keep me from attending the Robot Roundup."

Rico hunched his shoulders. "I didn't mean it that way. I wondered if you were doing a demonstration or anything."

"Oh, yes." Mr. Thompson waved toward the other side of the room. "I'm showing a new drone I developed. I guess you're competing without me this year."

"Yes," Naomi said.

After a long, awkward pause, Mr. Thompson said, "Well, good luck." He sighed and walked away.

When he was out of earshot, Naomi said, "He didn't seem happy to see us. And I don't think he really cares if we win or not."

"He must still like the Greenfield team," Violet said. "Why else would he be wearing your tee shirt?"

"I don't know," said Henry. "And I don't know how he knew our names. That whole conversation was pretty strange."

Trouble at the Trials

The children went on to the food court and found a table. Several robots moved through the room. The tops of the robots looked like androids, but instead of legs, they had wheels. One robot came over to the table where the children sat. It spoke in a high, cute voice. "Would you like to order?" It moved its arms as it spoke, and its eyes flashed green and blue. A computer screen on the robot's chest showed the food they could get. Everyone ordered sandwiches and drinks. Then the robot asked, "Would you like to charge this to the Greenfield STEAM Team account?"

"All these robots know who you are!" said Benny.

Rico said, "It must be reading the chips in our

ID badges, like SARA did."

"Please put the team orders on that account," said Henry. "Can I pay cash for our visitors?"

"Of course." The robot took the money, bowed, and rolled away. A few minutes later, it returned carrying a tray. The robot delivered the food, bowed again, and went to help other customers.

"This is so neat," said Benny. "All restaurants should get robot waiters!"

"Maybe someday they will," said Rico. "Some countries already use robot waiters—even robot cooks!"

They finished eating and put their garbage in the trash and recycling bins. Henry said, "Some of the teams are competing today. Let's watch."

The group moved to the big room that held the high school competition. Lines made from tape divided sections of the floor. In each section, groups of teenagers and adults gathered. The children paused to watch the first group. Large sheets of black paper were taped to the floor. A plastic block sat in one corner of the paper.

"What's going on?" Benny asked.

Jessie stepped closer to her brother and lowered her voice. "The robot has to move through the rooms of the house and collect something. The black paper acts like the rooms. The robot needs to go get that plastic block."

The robot, about a foot high and two feet long, moved across the paper with a whir of its motor. When it got to the edge of the paper, it backed up and turned. The robot explored the entire area. Finally it reached the corner with the plastic block.

The robot lifted its arms and squeezed them together. It lifted the plastic block and backed up. The robot headed back to the entrance with its prize. A judge announced the time the robot had spent on the challenge. The team members cheered and clapped.

The children moved on to the next group. Jessie told Benny, "Remember the theme, When Disaster Strikes? In a real disaster, robots can go places that aren't safe for humans."

"Because the robots are so little?" asked Benny.

"That's part of it," said Jessie. "Small robots can get through narrow places. If a building is damaged, the robots could go in first to study the area. Video cameras could show people what it looks like inside. In some cases, the robots might even be able to fix problems. They could move debris or cut through walls. Once it's safe, the people can go in."

"Could DogBot do something like that?" Benny asked.

"Not really," Jessie continued. "For this competition, the robots do pretend activities. Our goal is to get DogBot to go over or around objects. This teaches us how robots work. Maybe someday we'll work on real rescue robots. For now, the contest is about working together, solving problems, and having fun."

They watched another high school test. For this one, black tape made lines across a white floor. The lines turned and curved. A robot tried to follow the lines. Naomi explained, "This robot has sensors that can see the line. See the green squares in the corners? Sensors in the robot can see the color. The green tells the robot which way to turn."

The robot went off course and bumped into a

wall. The judge picked up the robot and placed it back at the start. "Let's try again from the beginning," she said.

The teenage team members whispered encouragement to the robot. An adult wearing the team T-shirt stood back, watching quietly.

As the children moved on, Jessie said, "Everyone is so nice. Even the judges are helpful. They want everyone to do well."

Rico said, "And there aren't a lot of parents yelling and telling their kids what to do."

Naomi nodded. "Adults aren't allowed to help in any way. Coach helped us prepare, but during the contest, we are in charge."

"How do they decide who wins?" Benny asked. "Is it the fastest robot through the challenge?"

"That's part of it," said Naomi. "For the student competitions, the judges look at the design of the robot, how well the robot handles the problem it is given, and teamwork. The judges watch how well we work together. They make sure everyone shares their ideas with respect."

"I'm glad!" said Jessie. "It's nice to work with a

team that's respectful."

"That's something Logan doesn't understand," said Naomi. "By being so competitive, he hurts his team. They always have a good robot. Last year their robot did the course faster than ours. He's right about that. But the Silver City team argued during the competition. I think that's why they didn't win."

Henry said, "That must be why Logan says the Greenfield team was scored wrong."

"Right," said Naomi. "He thought their better time from the challenge meant they won. He was really upset when they announced us as the winner."

"I wish we could help him understand what really happened," said Jessie.

They watched several groups take on the challenge. Then they wandered farther into the room. "Oh, look!" said Jessie. "Here are the middle school teams competing today."

In this test, the robots had to go over or around obstacles. The test area had walls, ramps, and dozens of plastic balls rolling around. "In a disaster, the robot has to get through rough terrain," Naomi explained. "This tests the robot's ability to do that."

The children crept closer to watch the group compete. Rico whispered, "This team took third place last year. Look how well they're doing!" The team members wore T-shirts that said, "Monroe Robot Wranglers." They cheered as their robot turned through a doorway. Then it headed up a ramp. Its large rubber wheels gripped the surface. The robot was almost too wide for the ramp.

"They've made it!" Jessie whispered excitedly.

Just then a wheel fell off the robot, and it tumbled off the ramp while the wheel bounced away.

The Monroe team groaned. So did many of the people watching. "That's too bad," said Rico. The others nodded.

The judge picked up the robot and the stray wheel. He brought it back to the Monroe team as they gathered around. "I don't understand it!" a boy said. "I tightened all of those connections this morning. How could it come loose so quickly?"

Jessie nudged Henry. "Look!" She pointed across the challenge area. Logan was standing on the other side, half hidden between a couple of other watchers. He grinned and pumped his fist as he watched the Monroe team.

Henry frowned. "Do you think Logan did something to their robot?"

"Would he really go that far?" Jessie asked. "Would he sabotage a robot to win?"

"I don't know," said Henry. "Let's follow him and see where he goes next."

They turned to the rest of their group. Before they could speak, Benny said, "Is it time for a snack? My tummy says it is!"

"We want to follow Logan," said Henry. "He looked a little too happy about that wheel falling off."

"You two go ahead," said Naomi. "I'm thirsty, so I'll take Benny to the snack area."

"I want to watch this next group," said Rico. "Let's meet in the snack area in half an hour. Then we'll have another half hour before we meet your grandfather. We can look at some of the other displays on the way out."

Everyone agreed, so Henry and Jessie hurried after Logan. "He was heading toward the main entrance," said Jessie.

"I don't see him," said Henry. "Wait, I think that's him."

They were careful not to get too close. They followed him to the staging area, where they had left their robot. "What is he doing?" Jessie asked.

"He seems to be arguing with SARA, the guard robot," said Henry.

"I wonder what they're saying," Jessie said. "If we get any closer, he'll see us. What's that he's holding? Is it a laptop?"

"I think so," said Henry.

Logan turned and stormed away. Henry and Jessie ducked behind the edge of a booth. Then they looked at each other. Henry said, "He didn't get past SARA."

"Maybe she can tell us what he wanted," Jessie suggested.

Once Logan was out of sight, they crossed to the doorway where SARA waited. The robot said, "Greetings Jessie Alden. Greetings Henry Alden."

Jessie asked, "SARA, will you tell us what Logan wanted?"

SARA blinked her yellow eyes. "It is against my protocol to give that information."

Henry said, "I guess that means no. Well, we can check on our robot."

He tried to step past SARA, but the robot moved in front of him. She said, "You may not enter with electronic devices."

"What?" Henry asked. "Do you mean my phone? But I came in with it this morning."

"The competition has started," said SARA. "Electronic devices are no longer allowed. Team members may not change or update their robot's programming. It could give an unfair advantage."

Jessie said, "That makes sense. We've seen some of the challenges. It wouldn't be fair if we made changes based on what we saw."

"All right," said Henry. "We'll leave our bags by the door." He smiled at SARA. "You will watch them, right?"

The robot nodded. "All items are safe with me."

Henry and Jessie checked on their robot. It looked fine. They tugged on the wheels to make sure none had been loosened. Finally Henry shrugged. "I still think we should keep an eye on Logan. And we should double-check our robot before we compete on Sunday. But we can't do anything else now. We still have a lot to see."

"It's time to meet the others soon," said Jessie. "Maybe Coach has arrived!"

"I hope so," said Henry. "That would be one more thing we could stop worrying about."

But when they got to the snack room, their teammates were alone. No one had heard from Coach at all.

GoneBot

In the morning, they still had not found Coach Kaleka. He did not answer his phone or return calls. Jessie said, "Where could he be? I hope he's all right."

"We can compete without him if we have to," said Naomi. "But I don't think he'd want to miss our trials. Surely he will show up for our competition."

"Maybe something happened to his phone," Henry said. "He might not have received any of our messages. Where would he go if he didn't know where to find us?"

"He might go to the place where we left DogBot," said Naomi. "Coach would know we'd go there at some point."

Grandfather dropped them off at the convention

center, and the children went straight to the middle school robot area. "Good morning, SARA!" Jessie said. She tried to look past the robot to see whether Coach Kaleka was in the room. It was too crowded to see everyone.

"Good morning, Jessie Alden," said SARA. She greeted the others as well. "Please leave your electronic devices outside."

Henry gave his phone to Violet. "We'll only be a minute," he said.

Henry, Jessie, Naomi, and Rico went into the room and looked around. They did not see their coach, so they went to the table where they had left DogBot.

The robot was gone!

The team stared at the empty table. "What happened to DogBot?" asked Jessie.

They hurried back to the doorway. Benny and Violet waited nearby. Henry went over to SARA. "Our robot is gone," he said. "Do you know where it is?"

SARA's yellow eyes blinked. "The Greenfield robot did not leave this area."

"Maybe someone moved it," Naomi suggested. "That is the kind of joke Logan would play." The children went back inside and searched all the tables. Then they met up by SARA.

"Our robot is not in this room," Naomi said. "SARA, our robot was stolen."

"That is not possible," said SARA. "This room is monitored at all times."

"Who monitors it?" Henry asked.

"I do," said SARA.

Henry turned to his teammates. "SARA must have missed something. But how could anyone walk out of here with a robot? With all the people around, someone would notice."

"What about at night?" Naomi asked. "The place must be nearly empty at night."

Rico groaned. "A thief came in the night and stole our robot!"

Henry turned back to SARA. "Did anyone enter or leave this room at night?"

"No one entered or left this room last night," SARA said.

"Did anything unusual happen?" asked Henry.

"I do not understand the question," said SARA.

Henry tried to think of a way to ask the question so the robot would understand. Finally, he said, "Did you record any noise or action between midnight and seven o'clock?" The convention center should have been closed during those hours.

SARA's yellow eyes blinked a few times. She said, "My records indicate a noise at twelve forty-three. I checked the room. No humans were inside."

Jessie asked, "What if the person did not have a name tag? Would you know they were here?"

"Yes," SARA said. "No humans entered this area last night. Only robots were present."

Violet frowned at SARA. She still did not quite trust a machine that knew so much. "Did you steal the robot, SARA?"

"My current programming does not allow me to steal," SARA said.

"So you never left this area?" Naomi asked. "Not even for a minute?"

"I am here at all times," said SARA.

"She doesn't need to eat or go to the bathroom," Jessie observed. "She has no reason to leave."

Benny looked at his brother and sisters. "Do we have a mystery?" he asked, grinning. He wasn't happy about the lost robot. But he loved a mystery!

"If we didn't before, we do now," said Jessie. "Let's look for clues."

The team members went back into the room. Jessie crouched to take a closer look around their table. "I found something!" She grabbed a small, crumpled piece of yellow paper. "It's another sticky note. It looks like it fell off the table."

Jessie smoothed out the paper. The teammates leaned in to read the small writing.

ROBOT RANSOM:

Place $200 in a paper bag

on the bench by the fountain

at 11 a.m. tomorrow.

"I can't believe it!" said Rico. "Someone took our robot, and now we have to pay to get it back!" He was breathing fast.

Naomi bit her lip. "Our challenge starts at noon tomorrow. If we don't get DogBot back by then, we will miss the competition."

Rico kept muttering, "I can't believe this is

happening. We don't have two hundred dollars."

"Maybe we can figure out who did this," Jessie said.

"It must be Logan," said Naomi.

"We don't know that for sure," said Jessie. "And if it was Logan, we still have to find our robot."

Henry nodded. "The note is on yellow sticky

paper, like the one we found here yesterday. It has the same red ink, and the handwriting is the same too. The letter *i* has a circle instead of a dot on top. Rico, do you still have that note?"

Rico stared at him for a moment before answering. "I might have stuck it in my backpack." He dug through his bag and pulled out the other note. He placed it on the table next to the ransom note.

"It is the same handwriting," said Jessie.

Naomi frowned. "I think I recognize that writing." She scratched her head. "I can't place it, but I feel like I've known someone who dotted *i*'s like that."

"The ransom note had fallen beside the table," said Jessie. "The one yesterday was stuck to the table. Why didn't the thief place this note on the table?"

"Maybe someone knocked it off the table by accident," Naomi suggested.

"Maybe," said Jessie. "But a sticky note should stick to the table. Also, the ransom note was crumpled into a ball. Yesterday's note did not get crumpled until we picked it up."

"It all seems very strange," Naomi agreed.

"I threw away the note from our hotel room," said Henry. "But I think that writing was different. I'll see if anything else is under the table." He got on his hands and knees. It was pretty dark down under the table, so he felt around with his hands.

A minute later Henry stood up. He held several pieces of plastic.

Rico gasped. "Those look like pieces of DogBot!"

Henry nodded. "I think they are. They must have gotten knocked off and bounced to the floor."

"Poor DogBot," said Jessie.

"Poor us!" Rico groaned.

Naomi shook her head. "It doesn't make any sense. If someone wanted to hold our robot ransom, why would they break it?"

Someone spoke behind them. "Hey, STEAM Team." They turned to see Logan grinning at them. "You know what steam is, right? Just a bunch of hot air."

Naomi glared at him. "Actually, steam is water vapor. Did you steal our robot?"

Logan's eyes widened. "What are you talking about?"

Naomi gestured toward the empty table. "Our robot is missing!"

Logan shrugged. "You blame me for everything. Why would I want your robot? Our team's robot is better. I wouldn't use your silly robot."

Naomi leaned closer to him. "What about ransom?"

Logan looked confused. "What about it?"

"You might take our robot if you thought you could get money for it," Naomi said. Rico nodded.

Logan shook his head. "That's crazy. Your robot isn't worth anything. Is this some kind of trick? I bet you know you'll lose, so you hid your own robot. You want an excuse to drop out. Well, it doesn't matter whether you compete. Silver City is going to win!" He turned and walked away.

The Greenfield team watched him go. Jessie said, "He didn't seem to know anything about our missing robot. But I wish we could get a sample of his handwriting to compare to the note."

Naomi sighed. "I don't know what to think."

"If Logan didn't take our robot, who did?" Rico asked.

"That is the big question," said Henry. "I guess we should tell someone what happened."

"I wish Coach were here," Jessie said, and the others nodded.

The teammates joined Violet and Benny outside the room and explained what happened. Then they looked for the judge for the middle school competition. They found her as she was about to start judging another team. The children explained their problem.

The judge frowned. "I don't know what to tell you. I'm very sorry that you misplaced your robot."

"We didn't misplace it!" Rico said. "It was stolen!"

The judge shook her head. "I don't see how that is possible. The room is guarded at all times. The robot security guards are very reliable. That's why we use them. We had some problems with human guards a few years ago, but robots never leave their posts. They cannot be bribed. They cannot be forced to do something wrong."

Henry said, "But couldn't a robot make a mistake? They aren't perfect."

The judge said, "The robots have sensors to

monitor activity. Even in the dark, they would know if someone entered the room. I don't see how someone could fool them. They are perfect guards." The woman smiled. "Plus, they are less intimidating than human guards. People enjoy them so much!"

Violet shook her head. SARA made her nervous, but she didn't tell the judge that.

The judge glanced at her watch. "I need to start judging this team."

"What should we do?" Henry asked. "We can't compete without our robot."

"You do not compete until tomorrow," the judge said. "I'll give you another set of supplies. If you rebuild your robot in time, you can still compete."

"We have to start over?" Rico asked.

The judge gave him a sympathetic look. "I'm sorry. That's all I can do." She pulled out a phone and called the check-in desk. A minute later, she said, "Your supplies will be waiting for you. Good luck."

The children headed for the check-in desk. "It's not so bad," Henry said. "We have the programming on our computers. We only have to rebuild the robot body."

"That will take all day," Rico said. "Maybe all night too."

"We can do it," said Naomi. "You are so good at building! And this time will be easier because we know what to do."

"I guess so," Rico said. "I hope we can remember everything."

"Why don't you two work on building the robot," said Jessie. "Having too many hands work on it would only make it more confusing. We'll work on the finding DogBot."

"Good idea, Jessie. If we find DogBot, we can use him tomorrow," Naomi said. "If we don't, we'll use the new robot."

Rico nodded. "I only hope we can do one of those things in time."

Too Many Questions

Naomi and Rico headed back to the hotel. The Aldens went to the food court. There they could sit at a table and make plans. Benny ran ahead and greeted one of the waiter robots. "Hello! Do you have ice cream?"

"Good morning," the robot said. "I have several flavors of ice cream." The robot turned to face Benny. "It is early in the day for ice cream. How about some healthy fruit?"

"It's never too early for ice cream!" said Benny. "But I like fruit too." He turned to his brother and sisters. "Can we share some fruit salad?"

"Order two servings," said Henry. "One for you and one for the rest of us." Henry paid the robot.

They sat down at an empty table. As they waited, a robot rolled by with a tray of lunch food.

"We could have had burgers!" said Benny.

Jessie ignored him and took out her laptop. "I'll make notes of everything we know so far," she said.

"We have a lot of questions," said Henry. "We still have not seen Coach Kaleka."

"Do you think something happened to him?" Violet asked.

"He said he would stay at the same hotel as us," said Jessie. "But he's not there, and he isn't answering his phone. Maybe the school knows where he is."

"But today is Saturday," Henry said. "No one will be at the school."

Their robot waiter dropped off their fruit salads. Benny dug into his. Violet took a few bites from the second container and then passed it to Jessie. Violet said, "You have been working with this coach for a while now. Is it like him to be so late?"

"He is pretty disorganized," said Henry.

"He was often late to our after-school meetings," said Jessie. "His classroom is on the other side of

the school. I thought he was late because it took a long time to walk that far."

"Even after he arrived, he wasn't ready to work," said Henry. "He often seemed confused about what we were supposed to do. Rico and Naomi sometimes knew things he didn't."

Jessie nodded. "But they have been building robots longer. Mr. Kaleka became coach after Mr. Thompson lost the job. I don't think Mr. Kaleka had built robots before that. He normally teaches history."

"It sounds like your coach could be running late," said Violet. "But this is very late!"

"Yes," Henry agreed. "Still, we don't compete until tomorrow. Maybe he thought he only had to come for one day. He might not realize we're here for the whole weekend."

"I'm sure we told him we were staying at the hotel for three nights," said Jessie.

Henry nodded. "But how many times did Coach Kaleka ask us about the dates of the conference? He couldn't keep them straight. Maybe he got mixed up on the number of days as well."

Jessie sighed. "I guess we can only wait. Even if we found him, Coach couldn't rebuild our robot. And I don't think he could make the judge change her mind. No one believes DogBot was really stolen."

"We know it was," said Henry. "We have to figure out how. I'm not sure Rico and Naomi can build a new robot in time. We need to find out who stole DogBot and get our robot back!"

Violet pointed at the laptop. "Put down SARA as a suspect. That robot gives me the creeps!"

Jessie chuckled. "I don't know why SARA would steal our robot. But I will add her to our list of suspects."

"Maybe she wanted her own robot dog," Violet said.

"I agree that SARA is a suspect," said Henry. "She was the only one who could get into the room overnight." He thought for a moment. "She said something strange. Remember, she said her *current* programming does not allow her to steal. She didn't say that she didn't steal DogBot."

Jessie stared at him. "You mean her programming might have changed? Could someone change it between last night and this morning?"

Henry shrugged. "Maybe. Or maybe she changed her own programming. Remember what Naomi said? Some robots can learn on their own. That's what artificial intelligence is."

"I still don't think SARA stole DogBot," said Jessie. "What would a robot do with two hundred dollars?"

Benny pushed away his empty fruit container. "If SARA did want her own robot pet," he said, "she probably wanted money to buy robot dog toys!" The others chuckled.

"What about the sound in the night?" Violet asked.

"That's right," said Henry. "Maybe someone did come in during the night. But how did they get past SARA? Those walls are tall. I don't think anyone could climb them. They're temporary, but I don't think one person could move them."

"What about a ladder?" asked Violet. "Someone could have used one to climb over the wall. No, wait. How would they get down on the inside?"

Henry said, "How about this? Someone put a

ladder against the wall away from SARA. They climbed up the ladder and dropped down onto one of the tables. They might have broken our robot by landing on it. That would explain the pieces we found."

Jessie frowned, trying to picture the room in her mind. "That wouldn't work. Our table was against the back wall. That one goes all the way to the ceiling."

"Oh, that's right," said Henry. "They'd have to drop down to a different table. It wouldn't explain how DogBot got broken. Anyway, would SARA have missed all that movement? The judge said the robot would know if a human were in the area. Maybe SARA has heat sensors or something."

"She must," Jessie said. "SARA insisted she would know if a human were inside. She knows the difference between humans and robots."

"If someone got in, how they did it isn't so important," said Violet. "We need to know *who* did it. Naomi and Rico seemed sure Logan was the culprit."

"He acted like he didn't know anything about

it," said Jessie. "But he also really wants our team to lose. And he tried to get in yesterday with his laptop. Maybe he came back later and found a way to sneak in! Has his team competed yet?"

"I don't think so," Henry said. "Why?"

"If they did, that would mean they took their robot out of the room to use it for the competition," said Jessie. "After they competed, Logan could have changed the programming on their robot. SARA would never know. She only makes sure we don't change the programming *before* we compete. Maybe Logan programmed his robot to do something to ours!"

Benny looked at her with wide eyes. "So it really could have been a robot thief!"

They all considered this for a minute. Finally Henry said, "It makes sense that someone used a robot to get into the room. But even if Logan's robot did something to ours, then what? How did he get the two robots out of the room?"

Jessie groaned. "He didn't. At least, I saw the Silver City robot there this morning. Wait, I'll look up the schedule for the contest." A minute later, she said, "Silver City competes tomorrow. Logan could not have changed their robot's programming yet."

"It's starting to look like Logan didn't do it," said Violet. "But then who did?"

Jessie made some notes on her laptop. "Some other things don't make sense. Why were pieces of our robot scattered under the tables? Why was the note crumpled up and on the floor?"

Violet sighed. "We have two good suspects. SARA and Logan. But neither of them seems to fit the clues."

"Maybe it was Watch!" said Benny. "Our real dog didn't like DogBot very much."

"That would be a surprise twist," said Henry. "But Watch is still back at home."

"Besides," Jessie said with a smile, "I don't think Watch has very good handwriting." She studied her laptop screen. "We must be missing other suspects. What about Mr. Thompson, the old coach? He was acting strange yesterday. He knew our names, but we've never met him. He was wearing the team tee shirt. It was almost like he was pretending to be on our team still."

"He did seem nervous around us," Henry said. "He kept fiddling with his name badge. But SARA wouldn't let him in the room with our robot."

"Maybe he managed to sneak in," Jessie said doubtfully.

"Twice?" Henry asked. "He had to get in on Friday to leave the first note and again last night to leave the ransom note."

"That's true," said Jessie. "But someone got past SARA. We need to talk to her again."

"Let's go!" Benny said, gathering up their garbage. "Then we can come back here and order lunch!"

They made their way back to the robot staging area. It was tempting to stop and watch the demonstrations, but they had a mystery to solve! When the children reached SARA, they greeted her politely. They knew she was a robot and didn't have feelings. Still, she seemed so human sometimes.

"SARA, we have a question," said Henry. "Can you tell us if Mr. Thompson was in this area yesterday morning?"

SARA blinked a few times. "I have no record of a

Mr. Thompson here yesterday. I do show a Lilliana Thomas, Silver City Gearheads coach."

Henry frowned and looked at the others. "It's strange that their names are similar, but it must be a coincidence. I saw the Gearheads coach, and she definitely wasn't Mr. Thompson in disguise."

Jessie addressed SARA. "Mr. Thompson was the Greenfield coach last year. Was anyone from Greenfield here, besides us?"

"Yes," SARA said. "Greenfield STEAM Team Coach Kaleka was here yesterday morning."

The children stared at each other. They had not seen their coach anywhere all weekend. Had he been there all along?

What had Coach Kaleka been doing all this time?

A Race for Answers

"Could Coach really be here?" Jessie asked.

"I guess he must be," said Henry. "But where? Why didn't he answer our messages?"

Jessie frowned. "Maybe his phone broke. Or maybe he responded to Rico in the last couple hours."

Henry pulled out his own phone. "It's hard to hear a call in this big building. I could go outside and call Rico."

"Let's walk back to the hotel," said Jessie. "It's easier to talk in person, and we can make sure he and Naomi don't need any help."

"We should bring them lunch!" said Benny. "I don't think they can get food at the hotel."

A Race for Answers

Henry ruffled Benny's hair and said, "Good thinking. We can order sandwiches and take them to the hotel to eat later."

Violet smiled. "That will be nice. It's quieter there. All these robots get on my nerves sometimes!" She quickly looked at SARA to see whether the android had heard her. Fortunately, SARA was helping other people.

The children headed back through the big room. Many people were demonstrating their robots. One man stood at a microphone talking about a robot on stage.

Benny said, "That robot has arms and legs like a person. That makes it an android."

The robot was built like a human, but it had a strange way of walking. It kept its knees bent more than a person would. The robot bent and picked up a box, turned in a circle, and put the box back down.

Jessie said, "Remember how it's hard for a robot to walk on two legs? That robot had to keep its balance while it bent down. It also had to grip the box so it wouldn't drop it—or crush it."

A robot the size of a large dog came onto the

stage. It had four legs and a long neck that bent and straightened. It grabbed the box in its mouth and backed up, pulling the box.

The android bent forward and reached for the box. The animal robot pulled it away. They played a game of chase around the stage. Finally the animal robot let go, and the android robot picked up the box as people cheered. The animal robot bent its front legs, dipping forward in a bow.

Benny laughed. "You should teach DogBot to bow like that!"

Jessie grinned. "Maybe we'll work on that for next year."

They kept going through the crowd. Benny slowed down to look at something. When the others waited for him, Benny ran toward them. He kept looking back and almost crashed into Henry.

Henry caught him by the shoulders. "Whoa! What's so exciting?"

Before Benny could speak, a humming sound grew louder. A dark shape flew through the air straight toward them! It buzzed past them only inches above Henry's head. "What was that?" he asked.

Benny pointed at the thing as it flew back the way it came. "A flying robot!"

"That's a drone," said Henry.

Violet stood on her tiptoes to get a better look. "What's it doing?"

"It looks like an obstacle course," Henry observed. "See, it has to fly through those rings set up on posts. The rings are not in a straight line, so the drone has to zigzag left to right, and up and down."

"I want to see!" said Benny. "Does the drone fly itself?"

"I think someone is using a remote control," said Henry. "Let's look."

They squeezed through the crowd. When they had a clear space, Henry moved Benny in front of him. "See," said Henry. "That girl is flying the drone. She almost missed that hoop!"

"It's okay. She went back to it," said Jessie. "She's good."

Just past the line of hoops, a basket sat on a table. The drone hovered over it. Metal arms with claws stretched out and grabbed a small ball from the basket. The drone flew back through a different line of hoops. The girl dropped the ball into a second basket and landed the flying robot on a table.

The man behind the table said, "Good job! You went through the obstacle course quickly. Only four minutes and twenty-three seconds."

"That man!" Benny pointed. "It's the old coach we saw yesterday."

"He's right," said Jessie. "It's Mr. Thompson, the Greenfield coach who got fired. This must be the drone he said he was demonstrating."

"He's not wearing his Greenfield STEAM tee shirt today," said Violet. Instead, Mr. Thompson had on a blue polo shirt.

"He forgot his ID badge," said Jessie. "Oh, wait, he has it on. It's tucked into his shirt. I was wondering how he got in without a badge."

They watched as Mr. Thompson wrote something on a yellow sticky note. He put the note on a board standing behind the table.

"Look at those yellow notes!" said Jessie. "They are like the messages someone left us."

"That kind of note is very common," said Henry.

"It might be a coincidence."

Mr. Thompson asked, "Who wants to try the drone next?"

"You try flying the drone," Jessie told Henry. "Keep Mr. Thompson busy while we look at the notes."

Henry waved his arm. "I would like to try the drone, please."

Mr. Thompson did not look happy to see the Alden children. His face grew red. Still, he nodded and waved Henry forward. Mr. Thompson explained how the drone worked. It was controlled by a program on a cell phone. With the phone, the user could make the drone go up or down, left or right.

Meanwhile, Jessie, Violet, and Benny crept closer to the booth. Violet pointed at the sticky notes on the board. "He uses a red marker. It's exactly the same color as the ransom note."

"What about the writing?" Jessie asked. "I think it looks similar, but it's hard to tell from here."

Violet glanced at Mr. Thompson. He was not looking at her, so she slipped behind the table to look at the notes. Then she hurried back to

Jessie and Benny. "The handwriting is the same! Remember, both of the sticky notes had tiny circles for the dots in the letter *i*? All of these are the same."

They turned to watch Henry and Mr. Thompson. The former coach said, "You must go through all the blue hoops on the way out. At the end, pick up one of the balls in that basket. You control the drone's arms like this." He made the drone fly low over the crowd. A tall girl was wearing a baseball hat. The drone dipped down and extended two arms to grab the hat from the girl's head.

The girl looked up in amazement as the drone hovered above her. Then the drone held out the hat to the girl, who took it with a smile as the crowd laughed.

Mr. Thompson told Henry, "Once you pick up a ball, fly back. Go through the green hoops on the way back. If you miss a hoop or drop the ball, you lose. If you make it back with the ball, I will record your time. The best time each day gets a prize."

Henry nodded and took the cell phone. Benny ran over to him. "Can I see what you do?"

"We'll do it together." Henry knelt next to Benny.

Mr. Thompson held up a timer and called out, "Start!"

Henry guided the drone through the blue hoops. It bumped into a few of them but got through. At the far end, Henry had Benny control the drone arms. It took them some time to pick up a ball. Then Henry guided the drone back through the green hoops as Benny bounced with excitement.

When Henry landed the drone on the table, Mr. Thompson checked the time. "Seven minutes and twelve seconds. Sorry, Henry Alden. I don't think you will get a prize."

"That's all right," said Henry. "Thank you." He and Benny joined the girls. "I have an idea," Henry said. "Let's get out of here and talk."

Benny said, "Don't forget lunch!"

"That's right," said Jessie. "We can talk in the food court."

They ordered sandwiches to go from the waiter robot and sat at a table. Jessie opened her laptop to take notes. "We think Mr. Thompson wrote the ransom note."

Violet nodded. "The ink on the notes in his display is the same color. The handwriting looks the same too."

"But how did he get our robot?" Jessie asked.

Henry said, "That drone gave me an idea. SARA was guarding the robots last night. She says no one went through the front door. She also says no human was in the staging area. But *something* got back there. Maybe it flew over the wall."

Jessie gasped. "You mean a drone?"

Henry nodded. "Mr. Thompson is really good with that drone. It even has a camera so he can see where the drone is going."

"Could he control the drone from outside the building?" Violet asked.

"I think he could," said Henry. "With the cell phone, he can control the drone from hundreds of feet away. He could have left the drone on overnight, left the building, and used the phone to fly the drone into the staging area. It could fly over the walls, since they don't reach the ceiling."

"I get it," Jessie said as she tapped on her laptop. "The claws on the drone held the ransom note.

That's why it was crumpled up in a ball. The drone dropped the note and picked up our robot."

"That's right," said Henry. "When it grabbed our robot, it broke off some pieces. They fell to the floor."

"And that's the noise SARA heard!" said Benny.

"It all makes sense," said Violet. "A robot really was the thief, but it was a robot controlled by a person."

"Have we really solved the mystery?" Benny asked.

"Not quite," said Jessie, studying her notes. "We still don't know what's going on with Coach Kaleka. And Logan still might be involved somehow. Plus, why would Mr. Thompson steal our robot for ransom? And there's one more question. The most important question of all." She looked around at the others.

Henry nodded. "How do we get our robot back?"

A Fishy Story

The Aldens found Naomi and Rico hard at work in the hotel room. "How is it going?" Henry asked.

Rico pushed his hair out of his face and gave a sigh of frustration. "Slowly, very slowly. I don't see how we can finish in time."

Jessie sat on the floor next to them. "What's wrong?"

"We left our design notes at home," said Naomi. "I guess we should have brought them."

"We didn't think we'd have to rebuild our robot," groaned Rico.

Benny looked at the pile of parts. "That doesn't look like DogBot."

"No," Rico agreed. "It won't bark either. We

don't have time for that. We'll be lucky to get the new robot working well. For DogBot, we tried many things to see what worked best. But we can't remember all our final decisions. We don't have time to try everything again."

"We can get a working robot," said Naomi. "But it won't be as good as DogBot. Not even close."

Violet unpacked the lunches they'd brought. "Why don't you take a break?"

As they ate, the Aldens told Naomi and Rico what they had learned.

Rico put down his sandwich. "You really think Coach Thompson stole our robot?"

"It looks that way," said Henry.

"Coach Thompson taught us a lot," said Naomi. "He helped us with the design for our robot over the summer. He was pretty mad when he got fired from coaching. Maybe he still believes DogBot is partly his robot."

"So he steals it and asks for ransom?" Rico asked. "Is he trying to punish us? We didn't fire him!"

Naomi shrugged. "Think about it. The note asked for two hundred dollars. That is half the prize money. Maybe Coach Thompson thinks he did half the work."

Jessie had her laptop out. "We still don't understand some things. SARA said Coach Kaleka came to the staging area yesterday. Could he be helping Mr. Thompson?"

Rico shook his head. "I doubt it. Coach Thompson was mad at Coach Kaleka for taking the job."

Jessie said, "Oh, I wish we knew what happened to Coach Kaleka!"

"How can we find the answer?" Violet wondered.

A knock came at the door. Rico jumped, and the others stared in surprise at the door.

"Grandfather should not be back this early." Henry went to the door and looked through the peephole. He turned to the others. "We're going to get some answers right now!" He opened the door.

"Coach Kaleka!" Jessie, Naomi, and Rico all spoke at once. They stared at the man standing in the doorway wearing a fishing shirt and hat.

"Hello," Coach Kaleka said. "May I come in?"

"Of course," said Henry. "We're glad you found us." He introduced Violet and Benny. They let

A Fishy Story

Coach Kaleka take the one chair in the room.

"Why are you dressed like that?" Benny asked.

Coach Kaleka put down his fishing pole and tackle box. "I'll give you a hint. When I got your messages, I came straight here as fast as I *cod*. I'll *bait* you thought I disappeared into *fin* air, and you wouldn't be *herring* from me at all this weekend. But I'm not that *shellfish*." He chuckled. "I'm *hooked* on fishing jokes."

Jessie smiled, but she had more important questions. "Did you forget the conference was this weekend?"

Coach Kaleka shook his head. "My memory wasn't the problem this time. I got an email about two weeks ago. It said the conference dates had changed. It gave the new dates as next weekend. That's why I got so confused. You would talk about certain dates. Then I'd go home and check my calendar, which had different dates."

"We talked about the contest earlier this week," said Rico. "You said you'd see us here Thursday night."

"I meant Thursday night of next week,"

Coach Kaleka said. "I'm sorry I wasn't here. I don't understand what happened. Something is definitely fishy!"

"We all got the first email about the conference," said Jessie. "That one listed this weekend, which was correct. Why did you get an email saying the dates had changed? None of us got that."

"It's a good thing!" said Rico. "We might have missed the whole conference."

Coach Kaleka pulled out his phone. A minute later, he showed them the email.

Henry compared it with the email he had received. "They are very similar. They both have the conference logo. But your email added the word *Correction* and new dates. And it's from a different email address. The two email addresses are almost the same, but this one has an extra letter on the end."

Naomi turned to Coach Kaleka. "I'll bet Mr. Thompson sent you a fake email."

"Why would he do that?" Coach Kaleka asked.

"We have a lot to tell you," said Henry.

It took a long time to explain everything.

Then Coach Kaleka helped answer some of their questions. "It looks like Mr. Thompson pretended to be me," he said. "First he sent the email with the wrong dates. He knew it worked when I said I was going fishing this weekend. I talked about it in the teachers' lounge at school. I said I would be out of touch all weekend."

"He knew you wouldn't get my messages!" Rico said.

Coach Kaleka smiled. "He wasn't quite right. I didn't get any messages yesterday, but this morning I went to a different river. I was able to check my messages. Boy was I surprised!"

"Thank you for coming so quickly," said Jessie.

"I'm sorry I missed all the excitement," Coach Kaleka said. "Let's see, where were we? Mr. Thompson came here, knowing I was out of town. He must have picked up my registration. That way he had my ID badge."

"Of course!" said Jessie. "It also explains why he wore a Greenfield STEAM Team tee shirt yesterday. He was pretending to be the Greenfield coach."

Rico jumped up and paced the small room. "No

one would be surprised to see him in that shirt. People would recognize him from other years. They wouldn't even look at his name badge. He used your ID to go to the staging area and leave the first note."

"That's why he was covering up his badge when we saw him the first time," said Henry. "I thought he was fidgeting because he was nervous. And when we were trying out the drone, his badge was hidden under his shirt. He didn't want us to see that he had a stolen badge."

"I guess I was wrong about Logan after all," said Naomi.

"Are you going to apologize to him?" asked Henry.

Naomi made a face. "I'm not sure I'll go that far. He still said some mean things. And he might have pushed the first note under the hotel room door."

"He probably did," said Rico. "We know he was here in the hotel. He was standing nearby when your grandfather said our room numbers." Rico checked the time. "Now what do we do? If we have to build a new robot today, it won't be as good. Can we get DogBot back from Mr. Thompson?"

"I don't know," said Coach Kaleka. "We still can't prove anything. If we tell him we know what he did, he can deny it. It's a fine kettle of fish!"

"It's what?" Violet asked.

"Sorry," Coach Kaleka said. "I meant it's a tricky problem."

"We might never get our robot back," Rico groaned.

"Don't give up," Coach Kaleka said. "There must be some way to find DogBot."

"Mr. Thompson doesn't know you're back," said Henry. "He doesn't know we figured out he's the thief. He might come to collect the ransom tomorrow. We need to catch him in the act."

Benny had been quiet during all the talking. Now he jumped to his feet with a smile. "We can do it! We're good at figuring things out."

"Benny is right," said Jessie. "We have a few hours to come up with a plan. Tomorrow, we'll rescue our robot!"

Search and Rescue

Sunday morning, they all met in the girls' hotel room. The new robot sat on a bed next to a laptop. Naomi was using her computer to add the programming to the robot. "We got the new robot working, but we won't have time to test it very much," she said.

"No matter what happens, I'm proud of all of you," said Coach Kaleka.

Jessie smiled at their coach. He might tell bad jokes, and he might not be a robot expert. Still, it was nice to have him back. He reminded them that how hard they worked together was more important than whether they won. Even Rico managed to smile at Coach Kaleka's words.

"What will you call your new robot?" Coach Kaleka asked.

"I know!" said Benny. "NotDogBot!"

They all laughed. "That is a good name," said Naomi. "At least we have a robot for the contest if we can't rescue DogBot. Now what is the plan to get our first robot back?"

Henry placed a piece of paper on the table. "Violet drew this map. It shows the park area in front of the convention center. Here is the fountain." He pointed. "That bench is where we are supposed to leave the money in a paper bag." Henry put a paper bag on the table. Something inside made the bag bulge.

"Where did you get two hundred dollars?" Rico asked.

"We didn't," said Henry. He opened the bag and pulled out a roll of toilet paper. "We'll leave this in the bag and close it up. Mr. Thompson won't know there isn't money in there."

Rico peered down at the map. "Do you think he will bring DogBot when he comes for the money?"

"We talked about that a lot," said Henry.

Jessie nodded. "We don't think he will come in person for the money."

Rico stared at them. "What do you mean?"

"It's too risky," said Jessie. "He must know we could be waiting and watching. He won't want anyone to see him pick up the money."

Naomi frowned. "Then how will he get it?"

Benny bounced up and down. "With his drone! You didn't see him yesterday. He's really good at flying that thing." Benny pretended to be a drone flying through the room.

"That's right," said Henry. "We know he can use his drone from a distance. The drone has a camera, so Mr. Thompson can see where it's going. It has arms to grab and carry things. We think the drone will pick up the bag and carry it to him."

"I get it," said Naomi. "But when he gets the bag, he won't find money. Why would he return DogBot?"

"Because we will follow the drone," said Jessie. "We need to catch him with the fake ransom. Hopefully he will have DogBot with him too!"

"Even if he doesn't, he'll know we caught him,"

said Coach Kaleka. "I think he'll give your robot back then. Mr. Thompson has been angry lately, but he's not a bad person."

Rico picked up the map and studied it. "The drone can fly. It might go up and over a building. How will we follow it?"

"We will spread out around the park," said Henry. "See the letters on the map? They stand for our names. That is where each of us will be. Benny and Violet will wait with Coach Kaleka in his car. If the drone goes very far, they can drive after it. We will communicate by cell phone."

"But there's one more thing," Jessie said with a grin. "We have a backup plan in case we lose the drone." She pulled something out of the toilet paper tube.

"Is that a watch?" Naomi asked.

"That's right," said Jessie. "We borrowed it from Grandfather. It's used for exercise. It keeps track of location. The drone will pick up the bag, and the map on Henry's phone will show us where the watch is!" She folded the top of the bag closed and sealed it with tape.

Henry looked around at all the others. "Is everyone ready? We should get in place early."

"Let's go rescue DogBot!" said Benny.

Benny and Violet went with Coach Kaleka to his car. Benny had snacks and games to keep himself busy. Coach Kaleka told Violet about the wild animals he had seen on his fishing trip. Violet told him about their dog, Watch. Coach Kaleka said, "I get it—he's a *watch*-dog!"

"That's right!" Violet said.

Coach Kaleka grinned. "I'm *paw*-sitive he's your best friend *fur*-ever!"

The older children walked to the park and found hiding places. A few minutes before 11:00 a.m., Henry got ready to drop off the paper bag. They hadn't wanted to leave it earlier, since someone might have thought the bag was garbage and have thrown it away. Henry made sure his cell phone was showing where the exercise watch was. He crossed the park and put the bag on the bench. He paused and looked around. No one was paying any attention to him.

Henry walked to the convention center. He

stopped just inside the doors and looked at his phone. It showed where the bag was sitting on the bench. He peered through the large window next to the doors. Henry could see the bench, but the bag was hidden by the back of the bench.

At the other side of the park, Jessie sat in a corner behind a big planter. Peeking over the planter, she scanned the sky. Was that the drone? No, it was only a seagull. A tiny speck moved high above. That must be an airplane.

What if Mr. Thompson didn't come? What if he changed his mind about the ransom? Or what if it was all a trick to keep them out of the contest? They were supposed to compete in one hour!

A faint humming sound grew louder. Jessie looked straight up. The drone flew over the building, appearing right above her! She pressed back into the corner.

As the drone kept going toward the bench, Jessie gave a sigh of relief. The camera was pointed slightly forward, not straight down. It must not have seen her.

The drone hovered over the bench and turned in

a circle. Jessie ducked behind the planter when the drone's camera turned toward her. A few seconds later, she looked out again.

The drone rose above the bench with the paper bag in its arms. The first part of their plan had worked!

The drone swung toward Jessie again. She dropped down and pressed tightly against the planter. Of course, maybe it didn't matter now if Mr. Thompson saw her. He would think she couldn't chase the drone.

The flying robot disappeared over the roof. Jessie jumped up and ran across the park to meet Henry. He said, "I called Rico. I told him the drone went in his direction."

Jessie and Henry raced around the building. A figure was jogging down the block away from them. "There's Rico!" said Jessie.

Henry spoke again into his phone. "Naomi, we're going west. Join Coach in his car." Naomi had been waiting in the other direction. She would have trouble catching them on foot.

Henry and Jessie ran after Rico. A few blocks

away, they caught up to him at the edge of a park. The three of them stood, panting. Rico said, "The drone came this far, but then I lost it."

Henry checked his phone. The map showed the drone very close. "It's on the other side of this park."

They ran across the park. At the far side, they stopped and looked around. Several children played in the playground while parents waited on the benches nearby. A small parking lot held a dozen cars. Henry said, "The map shows the drone in the parking lot."

"I don't see the drone or Mr. Thompson," said Jessie. "Wait, that car trunk is open." She pointed to a gray car not far away. The car was facing them, so with the trunk open, they couldn't see whether anyone was behind it. They walked toward the car.

Suddenly the drone flew up from behind the car. It held something large in its arms. A man stepped into view next to the car. Rico yelled, "It's Mr. Thompson!"

Mr. Thompson jumped and dropped something he was holding. He stared at the children for several seconds. Then he spun and ran away.

The Robot Ransom

Rico dashed after Mr. Thompson. Jessie called Coach Kaleka and told him where they were. Henry ran into the parking lot, but he was not chasing Mr. Thompson. He watched the drone because he had seen what it was holding.

The drone flew up high and then dropped down again. It headed straight toward Henry. He got ready to grab it, but the drone jerked sideways before it reached him. Henry's fingers gripped empty air.

Now the drone was heading toward Jessie. But she was talking on the phone and looking the other way. Henry yelled, "Look out!"

Jessie spun around. Her eyes widened as the drone came straight at her. She ducked just in time.

The drone disappeared into the branches of a tree. *Crash!* The trees branches shook, and leaves dropped to the ground. A moment later, something fell out of the tree.

Henry and Jessie ran to the tree. They stared at the thing on the ground. "Oh no," Jessie whispered.

DogBot lay in pieces on the ground.

A few minutes later the other children joined

them. Mr. Thompson and Coach Kaleka came too. They all stared at the mess under the tree.

Henry dropped to his knees. "Our robot! It's ruined!"

Split Decision

"I'm sorry," said Mr. Thompson. "I didn't mean for this to happen." He looked up into the tree. "My drone must be stuck in the tree. It's probably broken too. I was trying to return your robot, but when you yelled, you startled me. I dropped the controls, and the drone went wild."

Coach Kaleka boosted Henry into the tree. Henry was able to grab the drone and bring it down.

Mr. Thompson looked at the drone's twisted arms and let out a long sigh. "Oh well. I guess I deserve this. Anyway, here is your money." He held out the paper bag.

Jessie took the bag, which was still taped closed.

"Did you open the bag?"

"No," said Mr. Thompson. "I was going to leave it at the conference check-in table for you. I decided I didn't want the money. I only wanted to scare everyone for a little while."

"Scaring people is not nice!" said Benny.

Mr. Thompson's face went red. "I know it isn't. I was so mad about getting fired from coaching. I thought I deserved some credit for the work I did." He looked at Rico and Naomi. "I did help you get to the regional tournament, right?"

They both nodded. Naomi said, "You helped a lot. But *we* didn't fire you."

"You're right," Mr. Thompson said. "It wasn't your fault, and I shouldn't have tried to punish you. I let my anger get the best of me. I will tell the judges how I stole and broke your robot."

Naomi smiled at him. "I'm glad we found out the truth. The scary part was not knowing why this was happening."

Rico checked the time. "We only have half an hour until we compete. And no DogBot!"

"Pick up the pieces," said Coach Kaleka. "We

need to go back to the conference center. You will compete with your new robot."

Rico sighed. "It's not as good."

Coach Kaleka patted him on the shoulder. "You did your best. That's what matters."

Mr. Thompson said, "You're right. Doing your best is what matters. I had forgotten that. I guess you are a good coach after all." He held out his hand, and Coach Kaleka shook it.

They hurried back to the conference. The Silver City team was just finishing their test. The judge announced their time for the obstacle course. "Seventeen minutes and twelve seconds! That is the best time so far. The Silver City Gearheads also got through every obstacle. Good job."

The team members cheered. Logan spotted the Greenfield team watching and pointed at them. "Ha! You'll never beat us. This year the Gearheads are cooking up a win, and you're going to vanish in a puff of steam!" He did a little dance.

"Congratulations on your time," said Henry. He knew arguing with Logan would not help anyone.

The Greenfield team began getting ready for

their test. Meanwhile, Mr. Thompson and Coach Kaleka talked to the judge. They explained everything that had happened.

The judge smiled at the Greenfield team. "You've had a very exciting morning. Well, let's see what your new robot can do."

Henry placed the robot at the start of the obstacle course. He turned to his teammates. "Let's do this." They all bumped fists.

The judge held up her timer. "Start!" Naomi flicked the switch to turn on the robot.

NotDogBot moved in a straight line but then turned too soon and clipped a wall. Then around the next curve it turned a little too late.

"It keeps missing the turns," said Henry.

Naomi sighed. "I think the timing is off with the new body."

"You worked so hard on that for DogBot," said Jessie. "We must have tested it a hundred times." After several tries, NotDogBot made it through a doorway.

The next section had lots of colored balls. NotDogBot tried to use its mechanical arms to push balls out of the way. Several times a ball got stuck under the robotic arm. "That's my fault," said Rico. "The joints seemed stiff yesterday. But I didn't have anything to help them slide."

Minutes ticked past. Finally the robot got through the room. Everyone let out a sigh of relief.

Next the robot had to go over a pile of rocks. NotDogBot slowly crawled up the rocks. The pile shifted, and the robot slid backward. One wheel got caught between two rocks. Rico stared at NotDogBot as if he could move the robot with his mind. The robot rocked forward and backward on the rocks.

"It's doing exactly what it's supposed to!" said Jessie. "I remember how hard we worked on the programming for this. It was so much harder than simply getting DogBot to go forward."

Finally NotDogBot freed its wheel. It reached the top of the pile and went down the other side.

Rico wiped sweat from his forehead. They were getting close to the end of the obstacle course.

NotDogBot reached a ramp. "It's not aimed right!" said Jessie.

"It's all right," said Henry. "Its sensors saw the problem. Remember, we planned for this kind of thing. It's backing up and getting lined up." Everyone whispered encouragement to the robot.

But at the top of the ramp, one of NotDogBot's wheels slid off the side. The wheel spun and spun in the air. NotDogBot could not go forward or backward.

Finally Naomi said, "I think it's stuck for good."

The judge said, "You are out of time."

"Yes!" Logan pumped his fist and gave his teammates high fives.

Jessie said, "We got pretty far." She turned to Rico and Naomi. "I'm so impressed you built NotDogBot in less than a day!" The Greenfield team members all congratulated one another. Coach Kaleka beamed with pride.

The judge said, "Good job. We will announce the winners shortly." She joined some other people, and they talked for a while. Finally the judge got on stage and asked for everyone's attention. "We have an unusual situation today. We have two winners. We are going to award the prize money to the Silver

City Gearheads." The Silver City team ran to the stage. The judge added, "But the trophy goes to the Greenfield STEAM Team."

"What?" Logan exclaimed. "But we won fair and square! We had the best robot and the best time. Greenfield didn't even finish."

The Greenfield team members slowly walked onto the stage. They could hardly believe what they had heard.

The judge shook them each by the hand. Then she turned to the audience and said, "We hope young people will learn a lot by building robots. We judge the teams based on many things. Completing the course quickly is only part of the test. The point of this contest is to use technology to solve real problems. The Greenfield team did that better than any other team. They faced a problem when their robot was stolen, and they showed great creativity and teamwork in trying to solve that problem."

Jessie, Henry, Naomi, and Rico grinned. Violet and Benny waved from the audience.

The Silver City coach stepped forward. "What about the national competition?" she asked.

Split Decision

The judge said, "Silver City will advance to the national tournament. They showed excellent robotics skills. They also worked well as a team." She looked at Logan and added, "Even if they did not always show good sportsmanship to other teams. Keep working on that."

The judge handed the trophy to Naomi. "The trophy goes to Greenfield. I hope it will help them remember their hard work and success."

The teams left the stage as people cheered. Violet and Benny admired the trophy. The Silver City team caught up to the Greenfield group. Logan said, "Hey, wait a minute. What was that about your robot being stolen? Was that really true?"

Naomi and Rico took turns explaining what had happened. Soon they were chatting cheerfully with the Gearheads.

Henry's phone rang. "It's Grandfather!" He pulled his siblings aside and answered the call. He put the phone on speaker so they could all hear.

"The contest is over, right?" Grandfather asked. "How did it go?"

"Great!" said Henry.

Jessie laughed. "We didn't win the money." She looked at the trophy. Then she looked at her teammates, who were now also her good friends. "But we got something worth more than four hundred dollars."

"Oh? It sounds like you have a story," said Grandfather. "Tell me all about it tonight. I'll see you soon." They agreed and said good-bye.

"Now you have DogBot and NotDogBot," said Violet. "But I miss our not-bot dog, Watch. I'm glad we're going home tonight."

"Me too," said Jessie. "But first we should celebrate."

"The best way to celebrate is with ice cream!" said Benny. He held up the trophy with a grin. "This thing is nice, but dessert is what I call a prize!"

Turn the page to read
a sneak preview of

THE DOUGHNUT
WHODUNIT

the next
Boxcar Children mystery!

"Woah! Look at that!" said Benny. He pointed across Main Street, where people were standing in a line that stretched far down the sidewalk.

"I wonder what they're waiting for," said Jessie. She read aloud from the colorful sign. "'The Donut Dispensary.' That place wasn't here the last time we came into town."

"Another doughnut shop!" said Benny. "That makes two in Greenfield!"

The Alden children crossed the street. But when they got to the store, they couldn't see very much. The crowd of people was too thick to see into the window or doorway.

"Maybe we should come back later when the line isn't so long," said Henry.

Violet agreed. "Even if people think this place is so great, I can't believe their doughnuts are better than the ones they make at Delilah's Doughnut

Shop. And there's never a line like this there."

"These doughnuts look crazy!" said Benny, coming out of the crowd. "I ducked down and got close to the window, and I saw one that had bacon and syrup on it!"

"I don't know if that sounds great or terrible." Jessie chuckled. "But I am curious what other kinds they have."

"It doesn't look like there's any place to sit," said Henry.

"That's weird," said Violet. "I like to sit down and enjoy my food, like we do at Delilah's."

"I agree," said Jessie. "Why don't we go see what's going on there?"

"And get some doughnuts!" said Benny. "Do you think they have ones with bacon and syrup?"

"Oh, Benny," said Jessie. "You know the real attraction is our friends, Dawn and Steve. I wonder how they feel about the new doughnut shop in town."

The children turned to leave, but a tall, thin delivery man in a brown uniform was right behind them. He had a two-wheeled hand truck loaded with boxes and was trying to get through the crowd.

"Sorry, folks," he said. "Sorry. I need to get in the door. Thanks for moving aside."

As the Aldens stepped to the side, one of the boxes started to fall and Henry caught it.

"Woah, nice reflexes, young man," the delivery man said. "Thanks for the help."

"No problem," said Henry, setting the box back onto the stack. "Do you need help getting that inside?"

The delivery man shook his head. "I should be able to weave my way in. Thanks again."

As the man disappeared into the crowd, the Aldens continued on their way. It was only a few blocks to Delilah's.

At the shop, it looked like both Steve and Dawn were extra busy, even though the store wasn't full of customers. The Aldens left their jackets at a table and went up to the counter. On the racks were signs with the names of each kind of doughnut: glazed, powdered sugar dunkers, chocolate dunkers, jelly doughnuts, and Delilah's Classic Buttermilk Dollie Doughnuts.

"They all look so good," said Jessie. "I don't think I can decide. The chocolate dunkers are kind of gooey in a great way. And the buttermilk ones are so puffy and tasty. And then there are the glazed ones that practically melt in your mouth. Mmmm."

"We could each order a different one and share them," suggested Violet.

"You guys can do that," said Benny. "I want one of each!"

Henry, Violet, and Jessie laughed. "You can order one, Benny," said Henry. "We can each pick our own favorite. And let's get some milk too."

All this time, Steve hurried to and fro, carrying trays of doughnuts from the back room. When he saw the Aldens, he smiled and waved at them, and then he hurried away.

"Poor Steve," said Dawn, after she took the children's orders. "Our apprentice baker quit last week, and we don't have a replacement yet. We have more work than we can keep up with right now."

"Why did he quit?" asked Benny. "I think it would be fun to work here."

Dawn sighed and looked down. "I wish I knew

why he quit. Nathan was such a good worker, even though he and Steve sometimes disagreed. He told us he was leaving only three days before he went. That's not enough time to find a good replacement." Dawn looked frustrated and a little sad.

"We can help, Dawn," offered Henry. "We're on spring break now. We can do lots of things for you this week." The other children nodded.

"That would be such a big help!" said Dawn. "But are you kids sure you want to be helping out here while you're on break?"

"What could be better than being surrounded by doughnuts?" asked Benny.

"Great!" said Dawn. "But first, have your doughnuts. I'll come over to your table when things quiet down."

While they waited, the children ate their doughnuts and looked around the familiar shop.

"This shop feels happy," said Benny as he wiped crumbs from his mouth.

Henry laughed. "I think you mean that you feel happy being here, Benny," he said.

"Delilah's has lots of happy customers," said

Jessie. "Most of them stay and chat with each other."

"I like hanging out here too. The old photos and posters are so interesting," said Violet. "They seem like old friends I'm visiting."

Dawn was just passing by with her coffeepot. "Have you seen the new doughnut shop yet? My friend Hilda Ramirez is the owner."

"Your friend owns The Donut Dispensary?" asked Henry. "Aren't you worried that her store will take away your customers?"

"I don't think that will happen," said Dawn. "Our shops are different in many ways. I think Hilda will find her own customers. Besides, people who come to Delilah's are very loyal. We always have the same five favorite doughnuts and the best coffee in town. More important, we give them a lot more than just doughnuts and coffee."

Dawn's big, warm smile got even bigger.

"What do you mean more than doughnuts and coffee?" asked Violet.

"You know," said Henry. "Like Benny's happy feeling. Right, Dawn?"

"Exactly!" said Dawn.

The door banged open. "Oh! It's Charlie," she said. "I have to go." Dawn hurried to help hold open the door.

"That's the same delivery man we saw at The Donut Dispensary," whispered Henry.

The tall, thin man in the brown uniform frowned as he wheeled his hand truck through the door. He seemed to be complaining to Dawn, who was helping him. The hand truck banged into Jessie's chair, and the delivery man swerved to avoid hitting Benny in the leg. The children heard the man grumble, "If you'd just clear a path to the back instead of having all these tables here, I wouldn't have so much trouble getting my hand truck through the room!"

The Aldens watched the man push his hand truck toward the back room.

"That was strange," said Jessie. "That man seemed so nice when we saw him at the other doughnut shop."

"He was nice," said Henry. "But not now. Not here."

The Boxcar Children 20-Book Set includes Gertrude
Chandler Warner's original nineteen books,
plus an all-new activity book, stickers,
and a magnifying glass!

978-0-8075-0847-3 · US $132.81

THE BOXCAR CHILDREN ®

GREAT ADVENTURE

An Exciting 5-Book Miniseries

Henry, Jessie, Violet, and Benny Alden are on a secret mission that takes them around the world!

When Violet finds a turtle statue that nobody's seen before in an old trunk at home, the children are on the case! The clue turns out to be an invitation to the Reddimus Society, a secret guild dedicated to returning lost treasures to where they belong.

Now the Aldens must take the statue and six mysterious boxes across the country to deliver them safely—and keep them out of the hands of the Reddimus Society's enemies. It's just the beginning of the Boxcar Children's most amazing adventure yet!

JOURNEY ON A RUNAWAY TRAIN
Created by Gertrude Chandler Warner

HC 978-0-8075-0695-0
PB 978-0-8075-0696-7

THE CLUE IN THE PAPYRUS SCROLL
Created by Gertrude Chandler Warner

HC 978-0-8075-0698-1
PB 978-0-8075-0699-8

THE DETOUR OF THE ELEPHANTS
Created by Gertrude Chandler Warner

HC 978-0-8075-0684-4
PB 978-0-8075-0685-1

THE SHACKLETON SABOTAGE
Created by Gertrude Chandler Warner

HC 978-0-8075-0687-5
PB 978-0-8075-0688-2

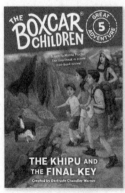

THE KHIPU AND THE FINAL KEY
Created by Gertrude Chandler Warner

HC 978-0-8075-0681-3
PB 978-0-8075-0682-0

THE COMPLETE FIVE-BOOK MINISERIES
Created by Gertrude Chandler Warner

Also available as a boxed set!
978-0-8075-0693-6 · $34.95

Hardcover US $12.99 · Paperback US $6.99

GERTRUDE CHANDLER WARNER discovered when she was teaching that many readers who like an exciting story could find no books that were both easy and fun to read. She decided to try to meet this need, and her first book, *The Boxcar Children*, quickly proved she had succeeded.

Miss Warner drew on her own experiences to write the mystery. As a child she spent hours watching trains go by on the tracks opposite her family home. She often dreamed about what it would be like to set up housekeeping in a caboose or freight car—the situation the Alden children find themselves in.

While the mystery element is central to each of Miss Warner's books, she never thought of them as strictly juvenile mysteries. She liked to stress the Aldens' independence and resourcefulness and their solid New England devotion to using up and making do. The Aldens go about most of their adventures with as little adult supervision as possible— something else that delights young readers.

Miss Warner lived in Putnam, Connecticut, until her death in 1979. During her lifetime, she received hundreds of letters from girls and boys telling her how much they liked her books.